Advance Agent

Christopher Anvil

Alpha Editions

This Edition Published in 2021

ISBN: 9789354599873

Design and Setting By
Alpha Editions
www.alphaedis.com
Email – info@alphaedis.com

As per information held with us this book is in Public Domain. This book is a reproduction of an important historical work. Alpha Editions uses the best technology to reproduce historical work in the same manner it was first published to preserve its original nature. Any marks or number seen are left intentionally to preserve its true form.

TABLE OF CONTENTS

I	- 2 -
II	- 7 -
III	- 14 -
IV	- 20 -
V	- 28 -
VI	- 36 -

Raveling Porcy's systematized enigma, Dan found himself with a spy's worst break—he was saddled with the guise of a famed man!

I

Dan Redman stooped to look in the mirror before going to see the director of A Section. The face that looked back wasn't bad, if he had expected strong cheekbones, copper skin and a high-arched nose. But Dan wasn't used to it yet.

He straightened and his coat drew tight across chest and shoulders. The sleeves pulled up above hands that felt average, but that the mirror showed to be huge and broad. Dan turned to go out in the hall and had to duck to avoid banging his head on the door frame. On the way down the hall, he wondered just what sort of job he had drawn this time.

Dan stopped at a door lettered:

A SECTION
J. KIELGAARD
DIRECTOR

A pretty receptionist goggled at him and said to go in. Dan opened the inner door.

Kielgaard—big, stocky, expensively dressed—looked up and studied Dan as he came in. Apparently satisfied, he offered a chair, then took out a small plastic cartridge and held it in one hand.

"Dan," he said, "what do you know about subspace and null-points?"

"Practically nothing," admitted Dan honestly.

Kielgaard laughed. "Then I'll fill you in with the layman's analogy, which is all *I* know. Suppose you have a newspaper with an ant on the middle of the front page. To get to the middle of page two, the ant has to walk to the edge of the paper, then walk back on the inside. Now suppose the ant could go *through* the page. The middle of page two is just a short distance away from the middle of page one. That going *through*, instead of around, is like travel in subspace. And a null-point is a place just a short distance away, going through subspace. The middle of page two, for instance, is a null-point for the middle of page one."

"Yes," said Dan patiently, waiting for the point of the interview.

Kielgaard pushed the plastic cartridge he'd been holding through a slot in his desk. A globe to one side lighted up a cottony white, with faint streaks of blue. "This," he said, "is Porcys."

Dan studied the globe. "Under that cloud blanket, it looks as if it might be a water world."

"It is. Except for a small continent, the planet is covered with water. And the water is full of seafood—*edible* seafood."

Dan frowned, still waiting.

"Galactic Enterprises," said Kielgaard, "has discovered a region in subspace which has Porcys for one null-point and Earth for another."

"Oh," said Dan, beginning to get the point. "And Earth's hungry, of course. Galactic can ship the seafood straight through subspace at a big profit."

"That's the idea. But there's one trouble." Kielgaard touched a button, and on the globe, the white layer vanished. The globe was a brilliant blue, with a small area of mingled green and grayish-brown. "The land area of the planet is inhabited. Galactic must have the permission of the inhabitants to fish the ocean. And Galactic needs to close the deal fast, or some other outfit, like Trans-Space, may get wind of things and move in."

Kielgaard looked at the globe thoughtfully. "All we know about the Porcyns could be put on one side of a postage stamp. They're physically strong. They have a few large cities. They have an abundant supply of seafood. They have spaceships and mataform transceivers. This much we know from long-distance observation or from the one Porcyn we anesthetized and brain-spied. We also know from observation that the Porcyns have two other habitable planets in their solar system—Fumidor, a hot inner planet, and an Earthlike outer planet called Vacation Planet."

Kielgaard drummed his fingers softly. "Granting the usual course of events, Dan, what can we expect to happen? The Porcyns have an abundance of food, a small living area, space travel and two nearby habitable planets. What will they do?"

"Colonize the nearby planets," said Dan.

"Right," said Kielgaard. "Only they aren't doing it. We've spied both planets till we can't see straight. Fumidor has a mine entrance and a mataform center. Vacation Planet has a mataform center and one or two big buildings. And that's it. There's no emigration from Porcys to the other two planets. Instead, there's a sort of cycling flow from Porcys to Vacation Planet to Fumidor to Porcys. Why?

"The Porcyn we brain-spied," he went on, "associated Vacation Planet with 'rejuvenation.' What does that mean we're up against? Galactic wants to make a contract, but not till they know what they're dealing with. There are some races it's best to leave alone. This 'rejuvenation' might be worth more than the seafood, sure, but it could also be a sackful of trouble."

Dan waited, realizing that Kielgaard had come to the crux of the matter.

Kielgaard said, "Galactic wants us to find the answers to three problems. One, how do the Porcyns keep the size of their population down? Two, what is the connection between rejuvenation and 'Vacation Planet'? And three, do the Porcyns have a proper mercantile attitude? Are they likely to make an agreement? Will they keep one they do make?"

Kielgaard looked intently at Dan. "The only way we're likely to find the answers in a reasonable time is to send someone in. You're elected."

"Just me?" asked Dan in surprise. "All your eggs in one basket?"

"In a situation like this," said Kielgaard, "one good man is worth several gross of dubs. We're relying on you to keep your eyes open and your mind on what you're doing."

"And suppose I don't come back?"

"Galactic probably loses the jump it's got on Trans-Space and you miss out on a big bonus."

"When do I leave?"

"Tomorrow morning. But today you'd better go down and pick up a set of Porcyn clothes we've had made for you and some of their money. It'd be a good idea to spend the evening getting used to things. We've implanted in your brain the Porcyn language patterns we brain-spied and we've installed in your body cavity a simple organo-transmitter you can use during periods of calm. Because the Porcyns are physically strong and possibly worship strength, we've had your body rebuilt to one of the most powerful human physique patterns—that of an American Indian—that we have on record."

They shook hands and Dan went to his room. He practiced the Porcyn tongue till he had some conscious familiarity with it. Then he tried his strength to make sure he wouldn't accidentally use more force than he intended. Then, while the evening was still young, he went to bed and fell asleep.

It was Dan's experience that everything possible went wrong the first few days on a new planet and he wanted to be wide-awake enough to live through it.

II

The next day, Dan left in a spacetug that Galactic was sending on a practice trip through subspace to Porcys. From the tug, he went by mataform to the lab ship in the Porcyn sea. Here he learned that he had only twenty minutes during which conditions would be right to make the next mataform jump to a trawler close to the mainland.

Dan had wanted to talk to the men on the lab ship and learn all they could tell him about the planet. This being impossible, he determined to question the trawler crew to the limit of their patience.

When Dan reached the trawler, it was dancing like a blown leaf in a high wind. He became miserably seasick. That evening, there was a violent electrical storm which lasted into the early morning.

Dan spent the whole night nauseously gripping the edge of his bunk, his legs braced against the violent heave and lurch of the trawler.

Before dawn of the next day, aching in every muscle, his insides sore and tender, his mind fuzzy from lack of sleep, Dan was set ashore on a dark, quiet and foggy strip of beach. He stood for a moment in the soft sand, feeling it seem to dip underfoot.

This, he thought, was undoubtedly the worst start he had ever made on any planet anywhere.

From around him in the impenetrable fog came distant croakings, whistlings and hisses. The sounds were an unpleasant suggestion that something else had gone wrong. Between bouts of sickness, Dan had tried to arrange with the crew to land him near the outskirts of a Porcyn city. But the sounds were those of the open country.

What Dan wanted was to go through the outskirts of the city before many people were moving around. He could learn a great deal from their homes, their means of transportation and the actions of a few early risers. He could learn from the things he expected to see, or from the lack of them, *if* he was there to see them.

Dan moved slowly inland, crossed a ditch and came to what seemed to be a macadam road. He checked his directions and started to walk. He forced the pace so his breath came hard, and hoped it would pump some life into his dulled brain and muscles.

As his senses gradually began to waken, Dan became aware of an odd *swish-swish, swish-swish*, like a broom dusting lightly over the pavement behind him. The sound drew steadily closer.

Dan halted abruptly.

The sound stopped, too.

He walked on.

Swish-swish.

He whirled.

Silence.

Dan listened carefully. The sound could be that of whatever on Porcys corresponded to a playful puppy—or to a rattlesnake.

He stepped sharply forward.

Swish-swish. It was behind him.

He whirled.

There was a feeling of innumerable hairy spiders running over him from head to foot. The vague shape of a net formed and vanished in the gloom before him. He lashed out and hit the dark and the fog.

Swish-swish. It was moving away.

He stood still while the sound faded to a whisper and was gone. Then he started to walk. He was sure that what had just happened meant something, but *what* it meant was a different question. At least, he thought ruefully, he was wider awake now.

He walked on as the sky grew lighter. Then the fog shifted to show a solid mass of low blocky buildings across the road ahead. The road itself disappeared into a tunnel under one of the buildings. To one side, a waist-high metal rail closed off the end of one of the city's streets. Dan walked off the road toward the rail. His eye was caught by the building ahead. Each was exactly the same height, about two to three Earth stories high. They were laid out along a geometrically straight border with no transition between city and farmland.

There was a faint hum. Then a long, low streak, its front end rounded like a horseshoe crab, shot out of the tunnel under the building beside him and vanished along the road where he'd just been walking.

Now Dan saw a small modest sign beside the road.

Care
High-Speed
Vehicles Only
—Swept—

Dan crossed the rail at the end of the street with great caution.

The Porcyn clothing he was wearing consisted of low leather boots, long green hose, leather shorts, a bright purple blouse and a sky-blue cape. Dan bunched the cape in his hand and thrust it ahead of him as he crossed the rail, for some races were finicky about their exits and entrances. The straight, sharp boundary between city and farmland, and the identical buildings, suggested to Dan that here was a race controlled by strict rules and forms, and he was making an obviously unauthorized entrance.

It was with relief that he stood on the opposite side, within the city. He glanced back at the sign and wondered what "Swept" meant. Then he gave his attention to the buildings ahead of him.

Low at first, the buildings rose regularly to a greater height, as far as the fog would let him see. Dan remembered the storm of the night before and wondered if the progressive heightening of the buildings was designed to break the force of the wind. The buildings themselves were massive, with few and narrow windows, and wide heavy doors opening on the street.

Dan walked farther into the city and found that the street took right-angle bends at regular intervals, probably also to break the wind. There was no one in sight, and no vehicles.

Dan decided he was probably in a warehouse district.

He paused to look at a partly erected new building, built on the pattern of the rest. Then he heard from up the street a grunting, straining sound interspersed with whistling puffs. There was a stamping noise, a *thud* and the clash of metal.

Dan ran as quietly as he could up the street, stopped, glanced around one of the right-angle bends. He was sure the sound had come from there.

The street was empty.

Dan walked closer and studied a large brass plate set in the base of a building. It looked about twenty inches high by thirty wide with a rough finish. In the center of the plate was a single word:

SWEEPER

Dan looked at this for a moment. Then, frowning, he strode on. In his mind's eye, he was seeing the sign by the road:

Care
High-Speed
Vehicles Only
—Swept—

Dan couldn't decide whether the word "Swept" was part of the warning or just an afterthought. In any case, he had plainly heard a struggle here and now there was nothing to be seen. Alert for more brass plates, he wound his way through the streets until he came out on a broad avenue. On the opposite side were a number of tall, many-windowed buildings like apartment houses. On the sidewalks and small lawns in front, crowds of children were playing. They were wearing low boots, leather shorts or skirts, brightly colored blouses and hose, and yellow capes. Walking quietly among them was a tawny animal with the look and lordly manner of a lion.

It *was* a lion.

As far as the rapidly dispersing fog let him see, the avenue ran straight in one direction. In the other, it ended a block or so away. Apparently the crooked, wind-breaking streets were only on the edge of the city.

Dan thought of the questions Kielgaard wanted him to answer:

1, how do the Porcyns keep the size of their population down?

2, what is the connection between rejuvenation and Vacation Planet?

3, do the Porcyns have a proper mercantile attitude? Are they likely to make an agreement? Will they keep one they do make?

To find the answers, Dan intended to work his way carefully through the city. If nothing went wrong, he should be able to see enough to eliminate most of the possibilities. Already he had seen enough to make Porcyns look unpromising. The rigid city boundary, the strict uniformity of the buildings and the uniform pattern of the clothing suggested a case-hardened, ingrown way of living.

Across the street, a low door to one side of the apartment building's main entrance came open. The lion walked out.

It was carrying a squirming little boy by his bunched-up cape. The big creature flopped down, pinned the struggling boy with a huge paw and methodically started to clean him. The rasp of the animal's tongue could be heard clearly across the street.

The boy yelled.

A healthy-looking girl of about twelve, wearing a cape diagonally striped in yellow and red, ran over and rescued the boy. The lion rolled over on its back to have its belly scratched.

Dan scowled and walked toward the near end of the street. On less advanced planets, where the danger of detection was not so great, agents often went in with complex, surgically inserted organo-transmitters in their body cavities. Unlike the simple communicator Dan had, these were fitted with special taps on the optic and auditory nerves, and the transmitter continuously broadcast all that the agent saw and heard. Experts back home went over the data and made their own conclusions.

The method was useful, but it had led to some dangerous mistakes. Sight and sound got across, but often the atmosphere of the place didn't. Dan thought it might be the same here.

The feeling that the city gave him didn't match what his reasoning told him.

He crossed a street, passed an inscription on a building:

Freedom
Devisement
Fraternity

Then he was back in a twisting maze of streets. He walked till the wind from the sea blew in his face.

The street dipped to a massive wall and the sea, where a few brightly colored, slow-moving trawlers were going out. Dan turned in another street and wound back and forth till he came out along the ocean front. On one side of the street was the ocean, a broad strip of sand, and the sea wall. On the other side was a row of small shops, brightly awninged, with displays just being set in place out in front.

In the harbor, a ship was being unloaded. Flat-bottomed boats were running back and forth from several long wharves. On the street ahead, a number of heavy wagons, drawn by six-legged animals with heads like eels, bumped and rattled toward the wharves. Behind them ran a crowd of boys in yellow capes, a big tawny lioness trotting among them. On the sidewalk nearby strode a few powerfully built old men, their capes of various colors.

Dan glanced at the displays in front of the shops. Some were cases of fish on ice. Others were piles of odd vegetables in racks. Dan paused to look at a stack of things like purple carrots.

A man immediately came forward from the rear of the store, wiping his hands on his apron. Dan moved on.

The next shop had the universal low boots, shorts, skirts, blouses and hose, in assorted sizes and colors, but no capes. Dan slowed to glance at the display and saw the proprietor coming briskly from the dark interior, rubbing his hands. Dan speeded up and got away before the proprietor came out.

The Porcyns, he thought, seemed at least to have a proper mercantile attitude.

III

Dan passed another fish market, then came to a big, brightly polished window. Inside was a huge, chromium-plated bar-bell on a purple velvet cloth. Behind it were arranged displays of hand-grips, exercise cables, dumb-bells and skipping ropes. The inside of the store was indirectly lighted and expensively simple. The place had an air that was quiet, lavish and discreet. It reminded Dan of a well-to-do funeral establishment. In one corner of the window was a small, edge-lighted sign:

**You Never Know What the
Next Life Will Be Like.**

In the other corner of the window was a polished black plate with a dimly glowing bulb in the center. Around the bulb were the words:

**Your Corrected Charge—
Courtesy of Save-Your-Life Co.**

A tall, heavily muscled man in a dark-blue cape stepped outside.

"Good morning, Devisement," he said affably. "I see you're a stranger in town. I thought I might mention that our birth rate's rather high just now." He coughed deferentially. "You set an example, you know. Our main store is on 122 Center Street, so if you—"

He was cut off by a childish scream.

Down the street, a little boy struggled and thrashed near an oblong hole at the base of a building, caught in a tangle of the mysterious ropes.

"A *kid*!" cried the man. He sucked in his breath and shouted, "*Dog*! Here, Dog! *Dog!*"

On the end of a wharf, a crowd of children was watching the unloading. From their midst, a lioness burst.

"*Here*, Dog!" shouted the man. "A sweeper! A sweeper! *Run*, Dog!"

The lioness burst into a blur of long bounds, shot down the wharf, sprang into the street and glanced around with glaring yellow eyes.

The little boy was partway inside the hole, clinging to the edge with both hands. "Doggie," he sobbed.

The lioness crouched, sprang into the hole. A crash, a bellow and a thin scream came from within. The lioness reappeared, its eyes glittering and its fur on end. It gripped the little boy by the cape and trotted off, growling.

"Good *dog*!" cried the man.

Men in the shops' doorways echoed his shout.

"A *kid*," said the man. "They have to learn sometime, I know, but—" He cut himself short. "Well, all's well that ends well." He glanced respectfully at Dan. "If you're here any length of time, sir, we'd certainly appreciate your looking into this. And if you're planning to stay long—well, as you see, our sweepers are hungry—our main store is on 122 Center Street. Our vacation advisor might be of some service to you."

"Thank you," said Dan, his throat dry.

"Not at all, Devisement." The man went inside, muttering, "A *kid*."

Dan passed several more shops without seeing very much. He turned the corner. Across the street, where the boy had been, was a dented brass plate at the base of the building. On Dan's side of the street, trotting toward him, was a big, tawny-maned lion. Dan hesitated, then started up the street.

There was a faint clash of metal.

Swish-swish.

A net seemed to form in the air and close around him. There was a feel of innumerable hairy spiders running over him from head to foot. The net vanished. Something wrapped around his ankle and yanked.

The lion growled.

There was a loud *clang* and Dan's foot was free. He looked down and saw a brass plate labeled SWEEPER.

Dan decided it might be a good idea to see the Save-Your-Life Co.'s vacation advisor. He started out to locate 122 Center Street and gave all brass plates a wide berth on the way.

He strode through a briskly moving crowd of powerfully built men and women in capes of various colors, noticing uneasily that they were making way for him. He studied them as they passed, and saw capes of red, green, dark blue, brown, purple, and other shades and combinations of colors. But the only sky-blue cape he had seen so far was his own.

A sign on the corner of a building told Dan he was at Center Street. He crossed and the people continued to draw back for him.

It began to dawn on Dan that he had had the ultimate bad luck for a spy in an unknown country: He was marked out on sight as some sort of notable.

Just how bad his luck had been wasn't clear to him till he came to a small grassy square with an iron fence around it and a man-sized statue in the center. The granite base of the statue was inscribed:

I DEVISE

The statue itself was of bronze, showing a powerful man, his foot crushing down a mass of snapping monsters. In his right hand, he held together a large circle of metal, his fingers squeezing shut a cut in the metal, which would break the circle if he let go. His left hand made a partially open fist, into which a wrench had been fitted. The statue itself, protected by some clear finish from the weather, was plain brown in color.

But the statue's cape was enameled sky-blue.

Dan stared at the statue for a moment, then looked around. In the street beside it, a crowd of people was forming, their backs toward him and their heads raised. Dan looked up. Far up, near the tops of the buildings, he could make out a long cable stretched from one building to another across the street. Just on the other side of the crowd was the entrance to the main store of the Save-Your-Life Co.

Dan crossed the street and saw a very average-looking man, wearing an orange cape, come to a stop at the corner and look shrewdly around.

Dan blinked and looked again. *The man in orange was no Porcyn.*

The man's glance fell on the statue and his lips twisted in an amused smile. He looked up toward the rope, then down at the crowd, and then studied the backs of the crowd and the fronts of the stores around him, the lids of his eyes half-closed in a calculating look.

A brass plate nearby popped open, a net of delicate hairy tendrils ran over him, and something like a length of tarred one-inch rope snaked out and wrapped around his legs. An outraged expression crossed his face. His hand came up. The rope yanked. He fell on the sidewalk. The rope hauled him into the hole. The brass plate snapped shut. From inside came a muffled report.

It occurred to Dan that Galactic was not the only organization interested in Porcys.

Dan looked thoughtfully at the brass plate for a moment, then walked toward the entrance of the Save-Your-Life Co., past display windows showing weights, cables, parallel bars, trapezes and giant springs with handles on each end.

He tried the door. It didn't move.

A clerk immediately opened the door and took Dan along a cool, chaste hallway to an office marked "Vacation Advisor." Here a suave-looking man made an offhand remark about the birth rate, took a sudden look at Dan's cape, blinked, stiffened, glanced at Dan's midsection and relaxed. He went through his files and gave Dan a big photograph showing a smiling, healthy, middle-aged couple and a lovely girl about nineteen.

"These are the Milbuns, sir. Mr. Milbun is a merchant at present. Quite well-to-do, I understand. Mrs. Milbun is a housewife right now. The daughter, Mavis, is with a midtown firm at the moment. The mother became ill at an awkward time. The family put their vacation off for her, and as a result their charge has run very low. If you can get to their apartment without being—ah—swept, I feel sure they will welcome you, sir." He scribbled a rough map on a piece of paper, drew an arrow and wrote "6140 Runfast Boulevard, Apartment 6B," and stamped the paper "Courtesy of Save-Your-Life Co."

Then he wished Dan a healthy vacation and walked with him to hold open the outer door.

Dan thanked him and went outside, where the crowd was now almost blocking the sidewalk. He forced his way free, saw someone point, and glanced at the statue.

The wrench in the statue's left hand had been replaced by what looked like a magnifying glass.

Dan had gone a few steps when there was a thundering cheer, then a terrified scream high in the air behind him. He turned around and saw a man come plummeting down. Dan gaped higher and saw a line of tiny figures going across high up on the rope. One of the figures slipped. There was another cheer.

Dan hurriedly turned away.

He had already convinced himself that the Porcyns had a "proper mercantile attitude." And he thought he was beginning to get an idea as to how they kept their population down.

IV

Carefully avoiding brass plates, Dan made his way along an avenue of shops devoted to exercise and physical fitness. He came to Runfast Blvd. and located 6140, which looked like the apartment houses he had seen earlier.

He tried the outer door; it was locked. When someone came out, Dan caught the door and stepped in. As the door shut, he tried it and found it was locked again. He stood for a moment trying to understand it, but his sleeplessness of the night before was catching up with him. He gave up and went inside.

There were no elevators on the ground floor. Dan had his choice of six ropes, two ladders and a circular staircase. He went up the staircase to the third floor, where he saw a single elevator. He rode it up to the sixth, got off and found that there was a bank of four elevators on this floor.

He looked at the elevators a minute, felt himself getting dizzy, and walked off to locate apartment 6B.

A powerfully built gray-haired man of middle height answered his knock. Dan introduced himself and explained why he had come.

Mr. Milbun beamed and his right hand shot forward. Dan felt like a man with his hand caught in an airlock.

"Lerna!" called Milbun. "Lerna! Mavis! We have a guest for vacation!"

Dan became aware of a rhythmical clinking somewhere in the back of the apartment. Then a big, strong-looking woman, obviously fresh from the kitchen, hurried in, smiling. If she had been ill, she was clearly recovered now.

"Ah, how are you?" she cried. "We're so happy to have you!" She gripped his hand and called, "*Mavis!*"

The clinking stopped. A beautifully proportioned girl came in, wearing a sweatshirt and shorts. "Mother, I simply have to get off another pound or so—Oh!" She stared at Dan.

"Mavis," said Mr. Milbun, "this is Mr. Dan Redman. Devisement, my daughter Mavis."

"You're going with us!" she said happily. "How wonderful!"

"Now," said Mr. Milbun, "I imagine his Devisement wants to get a little rest before he goes down to the gym." He glanced at Dan. "We have a splendid gym here."

"Oh," said Mavis eagerly, "and you can use my weights."

"Thanks," said Dan.

"We're leaving tomorrow," Milbun told him. "The birth rate's still rising here, and last night the charge correction went up again. A little more and it'll take two of us to get a door open. It won't inconvenience you to leave tomorrow?"

"Not at all," said Dan.

"Splendid." Milbun turned to his wife. "Lerna, perhaps our guest would like a little something to eat."

The food was plain, good and plentiful. Afterward, Mavis showed Dan to his room. He sank down gratefully on a firm, comfortable bed. He closed his eyes....

Someone was shaking him gently.

"Don't you want to go down to the gym?" asked Mr. Milbun. "Remember, we're leaving tomorrow."

"Of course," said Dan.

Feeling that his brain was functioning in a vacuum, Dan followed the Milbuns into the hall, climbed down six stories on a ladder, then into the basement on a rope. He found himself in a room with a stony dirt track around the wall, ropes festooning the ceiling, an irregularly shaped pool, and artificial shrubs and foliage from behind which sprang mechanical monsters. The Milbuns promptly vanished behind imitation vine-covered doors and came out again in gym clothes.

Dan went through the doorway Mr. Milbun had come out of and discovered that the Save-Your-Life Co. had a machine inside which dispensed washed, pressed and sterilized gym clothes for a small fee. The machine worked by turning a selector dial to the proper size, pressing a lever, and then depositing the correct fee in an open box on the wall nearby. Dan studied this a moment in puzzlement, guessed his proper size and put the correct payment in the box.

He put on the gym clothes and went outside.

For forty-five minutes, mechanical creatures of odd and various shapes sprang at him from behind shrubbery, gripped him when he passed holes in the floor and wound themselves around his legs as he tried to swim in the pool.

His temper worsened. He stopped to look at Mavis as she swayed, laughing, on a rope above two things like mobile giant clamshells.

Mr. Milbun shook his head. "Mavis, remember, we're leaving *tomorrow.*"

Just then, something snarled and lunged at Dan from the side. There was a flash of teeth.

Dan whirled. His fist shot out. There was a scream of machinery, then a crash and a clatter. An imitation monster with a huge jaw and giant teeth lay on its back on the floor.

Milbun let out a slow whistle. "*Dismounted* it. Boy!"

"A one-bite, too," breathed Mavis.

Mrs. Milbun came over and looked at Dan approvingly.

Dan had been about to apologize, but checked himself when the others smiled cheerfully and went back to what they were doing. This consisted of dodging, tricking or outrunning the various contraptions that lunged at them, chased them, tripped them, trailed, stalked and sprang out at them from nearly every place in the room.

Finally the gym began to fill up with other people. The Milbuns got ready to leave and Dan followed.

Dan lay in his bed that night and tried to summarize the points he didn't understand. First was the question of vacation. But he supposed he would learn about that tomorrow. Next was "charge." Apparently one went on vacation when his "charge" was low, because the vacation advisor had said, "The family put their vacation off for her, and as a result their charge has run very low." But just what was "charge"?

Dan remembered the flickering bulb in the store window, ringed by the words "Your Corrected Charge—Courtesy of Save-Your-Life Co." Apparently he had *some* charge, because the bulb had flickered. But where did he get it?

Then he thought of the waterfront and of the little boy caught at the hole. What was the point of that? And why did that produce such an uproar when, a little later, a grown man could get dragged out of sight on a well-traveled street and never cause a single notice?

Dan felt himself sinking into a maze of confusion. He dismissed the problems and went to sleep clinging to one fact. The Porcyns *must* be honest people who would keep an agreement, once made. On what other planet could anyone find a slot machine with no slot, but just an open box for the money?

Dan fell asleep, content that he had the answer to that part of the problem, at least.

Before it was light, he awoke to an odd familiar buzz inside his head.

"Dan," said Kielgaard's voice, small and remote.

Dan rolled over, lay on his back and spoke sub-vocally. "Right here."

"Can you talk?"

"Yes," said Dan, "if I can stay awake."

"Can you give us a summary?"

"Sure." Dan told him briefly what had happened.

Kielgaard was silent a moment. Then he said, "What do you think 'charge' is?"

"I haven't been in any condition to think. Maybe it's a surgically implanted battery, set to run down after so long."

"Too clumsy. What about radioactivity?"

"H'm. Yes, you mentioned a mine on the inner planet. Maybe they mine radioactive ore. That would explain why I have *some* charge. There's residual radioactivity even in the atmosphere of Earth."

"That's so," said Kielgaard. "But not every planet has it. I'm wondering about this other agent you mentioned seeing. He sounds to me like someone from Trans-Space. And that's bad."

"They play dirty," Dan conceded.

"Worse than that," said Kielgaard's tiny voice. "They recruit their agents from Lassen Two. Maybe that's a break. Unlike Earth, Lassen Two is nearly radiation-free. And Trans-Space doesn't use finesse. They'll pump Porcys full of agents loaded down with organo-transmitters. Visual, auditory and olfactory. They'll broadcast on every wave-length, suck out as much information in as short a time as they can, then either pull some dirty trick or slam the Porcyns an offer. That is, if everything goes according to plan.

"But meanwhile," he added, "one or more of their agents is bound to stand in front of a free 'Your charge' device somewhere in the city. Very likely, that agent will be radiation-free and some Porcyn, for the first time in his life, is going to see a bulb that doesn't even flicker. If the Porcyns are as scientifically advanced as we think, and if Trans-Space is as dirty as usual, there may be a rat-race on before we know it."

Dan lay gloomily still.

"Dan," said Kielgaard, "where were you standing in relation to the other agent? Did he come up from behind or was he in front of you when you reached the statue?"

"I was in front of him. Why?"

"Because then you were in his range of vision. *He* may not have noticed you, but his organo-transmitter would. The chances are you appeared on the screen back at Trans-Space headquarters. They record those scenes as they come in and their experts go over them frame by frame. Unless you happened to be behind someone, they'll see your image on the screen, spot you here and there in other scenes from other agents, study your actions and recognize you as an agent just as surely as you recognized their agent."

"Yes," said Dan wearily, "of course they will." He was thinking that if he had been more awake yesterday, he would have thought of this himself and perhaps avoided it. But he couldn't be alert without sleep and who could sleep in a heaving boat in a thunderstorm?

"This changes things," Kielgaard was saying. "I'm going to see if we can get a little faster action."

"I think I'd better get some more sleep," Dan answered. "I may need it tomorrow."

"I agree," said Kielgaard. "You'll have to keep your eyes open. Good night, Dan, and good luck."

"Thanks."

Dan rolled over on his side. He tried for a moment to remember how the other agent had been standing and whether anyone had been between them to block his view, but he couldn't be sure. Dan decided there was nothing to do but assume the worst. He blanked his mind. Soon a feeling of deep weariness came over him and he fell asleep.

In the morning, Dan and the Milbuns ate a hurried breakfast. Dan helped Mr. Milbun grease his rowing machine, weights, springs and chinning bar, so they wouldn't rust in his absence. Milbun worked in a somber mood. All the Milbuns, in fact, were unusually quiet for a family going on vacation. When they went out into the hall, carrying no baggage, they even took the elevator to the third floor.

"Better save our strength," said Mr. Milbun.

The street seemed to Dan to have a different atmosphere. People were walking quietly in groups, their eyes cool and alert. The Milbuns walked in front of the apartment houses Dan had passed the day before, and across the street he saw the place where the chiseled motto had read:

Freedom
Devisement
Fraternity

It was gone. Some workmen nearby were lifting a stone slab onto a cart. Dan blinked. The motto now read:

Alertness
Devisement
Vigilance

The Milbuns plainly noticed it, too. They drew closer together and looked around thoughtfully. Carefully keeping away from brass plates labeled SWEEPER, they followed a devious route that led to the statue.

The statue had changed, too. The hand that gripped the circle was now hidden by a massive shield. The other hand still held what looked like a magnifying glass, and the motto was still "I Devise." But the shield gave the whole statue a look of strange menace.

Across the street, near the place where Dan had seen the Trans-Space agent, stood several men wearing orange capes, barred black across the shoulders. Nearby, the brass plate opened and a man in work clothes handed out a box and went back in.

At a store entrance up the street, watching them, stood an average-looking man in a purple cape, his look intent and calculating.

Mavis glanced at the statue and took Dan's arm. "Devisement," she said, "they won't take you now, will they, before vacation?"

Dan kept an uneasy silence and Mr. Milbun said, "Of course not, Mavis. Where's the belt?"

Mavis glanced at the statue. "Oh."

Dan looked at the statue, then at Mavis and Mr. Milbun, said nothing and went on.

They came to a large building with a long flight of broad wide steps. Across the face of the building was boldly and sternly lettered, high up:

HALL OF TRUTH

Lower down was the motto:

> **"Speak the Truth—
> Live Yet a While With Us."**

V

On one side of the stairs as they climbed was a statue of a man, smiling. On the other side was an urn with a bunch of carved flowers lying beside it.

A big bronze door stood open at the top. They walked through into a large chamber with massive seats in triple rows along two walls, and a single row of yet more massive seats raised along the farther wall.

A bored-looking man got up from a low desk as the Milbuns sat down in three of the massive seats.

The man asked in a dreary voice, "Have you, to the best of your knowledge, committed any wrong or illegal act or acts since your last vacation?" He picked up a whiskbroom and pan and waited for their answers.

"No," said the three Milbuns in earnest quavering voices.

The man looked at each of them, shrugged and said boredly, "Pass through to your vacations, live law-abiding citizens." He beckoned impatiently to Dan, turned to scowl at him, saw Dan's cape, stiffened, looked hastily out to the statue framed by the doorway, relaxed slightly and inquired respectfully, "Is it time for you to go on vacation, Devisement?"

"It seems to be," said Dan.

"I think you should, sir. Then you'd be still more helpful if called."

Dan nodded noncommittally and sat down in one of the massive chairs. His glance fell on an ornamental carving above the big doorway. It was a set of scales held by a giant hand. In one pan of the scales sat a smiling man. In the other was a small heap of ashes.

"Have you," asked the bored man, "to the best of your knowledge, committed any wrong or illegal act or acts since your last vacation?"

He readied the dustpan and whiskbroom.

The Milbuns watched anxiously at a door in the back of the room.

Uneasily, Dan thought back and remembered no wrong or illegal acts he had committed since his last vacation.

"No," he said.

The functionary stepped back. "Pass through to your vacation, live law-abiding citizen, sir."

Dan got up and walked toward the Milbuns. Another bored functionary came in wheeling a cartful of urns. He stopped at a massive chair with a heap of ashes on the seat, a small pile on either arm, and two small piles at the foot. The functionary swept the ashes off and dumped them in the urn.

A cold sensation went through Dan. He followed the Milbuns out into a small room.

He felt an out-of-focus sensation and realized the room was a mataform transmitter. An instant later, they were in a spaceship crowded with thoughtful-looking people.

Life on the spaceship seemed to be given over to silent, morose meditation, with an occasional groan that sounded very much like, "Oh, give me just one more chance, God."

When they left the ship, it was again by mataform, this time to a building where they stood in a line of people. The line wound through a booth where the color of their capes was marked on their foreheads, thence past a counter where they received strong khaki-colored capes, blouses and hose, and new leather shorts and boots to replace those they were wearing. They changed in tiny private rooms, handed their own clothing in at another counter, had a number stamped on their left shoulders and on their boxes of clothing.

Then they walked out onto a strip of brilliant white sand, fronting on an inlet of sparkling blue water.

Here and there huddled little crowded knots of people, dancing from one foot to another on the hot sand and yet apparently afraid to go in the water. Dan looked to the Milbuns for some clue and saw them darting intense calculating glances at the beach and the water.

Then Mr. Milbun yelled, "*Run for it!*"

A slavering sound reached Dan's ear. He sprinted after the Milbuns, burst through the crowd in a headlong bolt for the cove, then swam as fast as he could to keep up with them as they raced for the opposite shore. They crawled out, strangling and gasping, and dragged themselves up on the sand. Dan lay, heaving in deep breaths, then rolled over and sat up.

The air around them was split by screams, laced through with sobs, curses and groans. On the shore opposite, a mad dog darted across the crowded beach and emptied people into the cove. In the cove, a glistening black sweep of hide separated the water for an instant, then sank below. People thrashed, fought and went under.

Dan looked up. On the wooden building beyond the cove and the beach was a broad sign:

PORCYS PLANET REJUVENATION CENTER

Dan read the sign three times. If this was rejuvenation, the Porcyns could have it.

Beside Dan, Milbun stood up, still struggling for breath, and pulled his wife and Mavis to their feet.

"Come on," he said. "We've *got* to get through the swamp ahead of the grayboas!"

The rest of the day, they pushed through slimy muck up to their knees and sometimes up to their necks. Behind them, the crowd screamingly thinned out.

That night, they washed in icy spring water, tore chunks of meat from a huge broiled creature turning on a spit and went to sleep in tents to the buzz and drone of creatures that shot their long needle noses through the walls like drillers hunting for oil.

The following day, they spent carefully easing from crevice to narrow toehold up the sheer face of a mountain. Food and shelter were at the top. Jagged rocks and hungry creatures were at the bottom. That night, Dan slept right through an urgent buzz from Kielgaard. The next night, he woke enough to hear it, but he didn't have the strength to answer.

Where, he thought, is the rejuvenation in this?

Then he had a sudden glimmering. It was the Porcyn *race* that was rejuvenated. The unfit of the Porcyns died violently. It took stamina just to live from one day to the next.

Even the Milbuns were saying that this was the worst vacation ever. Trails slid out from under them. Trees fell toward them. Boulders bounded down steep slopes at them.

At first, the Milbuns tried to remember forgotten sins for which all this might be repayment. But when there was the dull *boom* of an explosion and they narrowly escaped a landslide, Milbun looked at the rocks across the trail with sunken red eyes. He sniffed the air and growled, "Undevised."

That afternoon, Dan and the Milbuns passed three average-looking men hanging by their hands from the limb of a tree beside the trail. The faces of the hanging men bore a surprised expression. They hung perfectly still and motionless, except for a slight swaying caused by the wind.

Dan and the Milbuns reached a mataform station late that afternoon.

A very hard-eyed guard in an orange cape, barred across the shoulders in black, let them through and they found themselves in another spaceship, bound for Fumidor, the mining planet.

Dan sat back exhausted and fell asleep. He was awakened by a determined buzz.

"*Dan!*" said Kielgaard's voice.

"Yes." Dan sat up. "Go ahead."

"Trans-Space is going to try to take over Porcys. There's nothing you can do about that, but they've landed agents on Vacation Planet to pick you off. Look out."

Dan told Kielgaard what had happened to the agents on Vacation Planet, such as the "undevised" explosion and being hung up by the hands.

Kielgaard whistled. "Maybe the Porcyns can take care of themselves. Trans-Space doesn't think so."

"How did you find out?"

The tiny voice held a note of grim satisfaction. "They ran an agent in on us and he gave himself away. He went back with an organo-transmitter inside him, and a memory bank. The bank stores up the day's impressions. The transmitter squirts them out in one multi-frequency blast. The agent is poorly placed for an informant, but we've learned a lot through him."

"How are they going to take over Porcys?"

"We don't know. They think they've found the Porcyns' weak point, but if so, we don't know what it is."

"Listen," urged Dan, "maybe *we* ought to put a lot of agents on Porcys."

"No," said Kielgaard. "That's the wrong way to play it. If we go in now, we'll be too late to do any good. We're still counting on you."

"There's not very much I can do by myself."

"Just do your best. That's all we can ask."

Dan spent the next week chipping out pieces of a radioactive ore. At night, Kielgaard would report the jubilant mood of Trans-Space. On the following days, Dan would chop at the ore with vicious blows that jarred him from his wrists to his heels.

The steady monotonous work, once he was used to it, left his mind free to think and he tried furiously to plan what he would do when he got out. But he found he didn't really know enough about Porcys to make a sensible plan. Then he began trying to organize what he had seen and heard during his stay on the planet. At night, Kielgaard helped him and together they went over their theories, trying to find those that would fit the facts of Porcys.

"It all hinges on population pressure," said Kielgaard finally. "On most planets we know of, overpopulation leads to war, starvation, birth control or emigration. These are the only ways. At least, they were, till we discovered Porcys."

"All right," agreed Dan. "Grant that. The Porcyns plainly don't have any of those things, or not to any great extent. Instead, they have institutions such as we've never seen before. They have 'sweepers,' so-called 'vacations' and a rope from building to building. All these things cut down population."

"Don't forget their 'truth chairs,'" said Kielgaard.

"Where you either tell the truth or get converted to ashes—yes. But how does it all fit in?"

"Let's take one individual as an example. Start at birth."

"He's born," said Dan. "Probably they have nurseries, but we know they stick together as families, because we have the Milbuns to go by. He grows up, living at his parents' place. He goes with other children to school or to see different parts of his city. A lion—which he calls a 'dog'—protects him."

"Yes," said Kielgaard. "It protects him from sweepers. But most grownups don't need protection. Only those whose charge is low."

"Of course. The boy hasn't been on vacation yet. He's not radioactive. Apparently you have to be radioactive to open doors. At the apartment house, the boy comes in a small door to one side. The lions, or what resemble lions, like the children but don't like the sweepers. And the sweepers are afraid of them. All right. But what about when he grows up?"

"Well, for one thing, he has to use the regular doors now. And they won't open unless he's been on vacation. And if he hasn't been on vacation and if his charge isn't high, the sweepers will go out and grab him. That must be what that sign you saw meant. 'Swept' was a warning that there was no escape in that direction."

"I begin to see it," said Dan. "I was safe on that road because the birth rate in that section wasn't high. But in the city, the birth rate *was* high, so, to keep the population down, the standards were raised. Apparently the sweepers were fed less and got more hungry. People had to go on vacation more often. But what about the rope?"

"I don't think we really know enough to understand the rope," said Kielgaard, "but maybe it's a face-saving device. People who don't think they're in good enough shape to get through 'vacation,' and who don't want to die a slow death avoiding sweepers and waiting to go through locked doors, can go across on the rope. Or perhaps it's a penance. If a man has done something wrong and he's afraid to deny it in the truth chair, perhaps he's allowed to confess and go so many times across the rope as punishment. The people cheered. That must mean it's honorable."

"That makes sense," Dan agreed. "All right, but why don't they just ship their surplus population to the other two planets?"

"We've studied that back here," said Kielgaard. "We think it's because they wouldn't dare. They've got their little mainland allotted and rationed down to the last blade of grass. They can do that because it's small enough to keep control of. Now suppose they try to enforce the same system on a new planet with a hundred times the land area—what's going to happen? They'll have unknown, uncontrollable factors to deal with. Their system will break down. That statue of theirs shows they know it, too. The man in the blue cape 'devises' and his strong right hand does nothing but keep the circle—their system—from flying apart. What puzzles me is that they're satisfied with it."

"There's another point," Dan said, "but I think I see it now. They've got a caste system, but people must be able to move from one caste to another. There must be a competitive exam or some system of choice. The vacation advisor said Mr. Milbun was 'at present' a merchant. His wife was 'now' a housewife. And no one ever asked my name, though I told it voluntarily to Milbun. It was always 'Yes, Devisement,' or 'Is it time to take your vacation, Devisement?' There were no personal titles like 'Sir Moglin,' or 'First Magistrate Moglin,' such as we've encountered on other planets."

Kielgaard grunted. "That would explain the differently colored capes, too. No one would care if a man was a street-cleaner ten years ago. They'd see his cape was blue and give him immediate, automatic respect."

"Yes," said Dan. "That's it. And no one would dare *cheat* about the color of the cape he wore, because, regardless of his position, sooner or later his charge would be gone. Then he would have to go on vacation. And to do *that*, he *has* to sit in the truth chair and tell the truth or get incinerated." Dan stopped suddenly and sucked in a deep breath.

"What's wrong?" asked Kielgaard.

"*That's* the weak point."

VI

By the end of the week, Dan was able to pass through a door with a specialized type of Geiger counter in the locking circuit.

And by that time, Kielgaard had noted sharp fluctuations in the mood at Trans-Space. There had been an interval of wild confusion, but it hadn't lasted. Many more Trans-Space agents had gone to Porcys and Trans-Space seemed to be on top again.

The instant Dan stepped from the mines through the door marked "Out," he was rushed through a shower, a shave and a haircut, shoved into a truth chair and asked questions, given a new cape and clothes, and buckled into a glittering belt by a purple-caped man addressed as "Reverence." No sooner was the belt in place than all, including "Reverence," snapped to attention.

"Devisement," said a man in an orange-and-black cape, "we need your decision quickly. At home, men have usurped cloaks of devisement and given orders contrary to the public good. They wore belts of power, but did not die when their false orders were given. In the Central City, they convened a council, seated themselves in the Hall of Truth, and on the very first oath every single one of them present was thrown into the life beyond.

"Because the statue was already belted, men wearing cloaks of devisement *had* to give the orders. But now they were all gone. Looters roamed the streets, breaking in doors. These men were vacation-dodgers—out so long that they couldn't even make a charge-light flicker—and the sweepers cleaned up some of them. *But they killed the sweepers!* Devisement, I tell you the truth!"

"I believe you," said Dan.

"Thank heaven. Devisement, something must be done. A young boy passed and graduated to the devisement cape, but before he could take action, he was shot from ambush. We found an old man of the right cape out in the country, and when we finally convinced him, he rounded up one hundred and fifty-seven vacation-dodgers and executed them. We had things in order, but now a glut of lunatics in devisement capes and belts of power have burst into the streets. Their orders are silly, yet their belts don't kill them. They have no fear of the Truth. Business is stopped and men are hungry. The people are going wild. Strange boats have appeared offshore. Mataform transmitters of odd design are being set up near the shore. This cannot go on without breaking the circle!"

Dan's throat felt dry.

"Sir," said the Porcyn desperately, "you *must* devise something! What shall we do?"

A faint tingling at Dan's waist suggested to him that he choose his words carefully. One lie or bad intention and the belt of power would probably finish him.

He thought carefully. The total power of the Porcyn planet must be at least the equal of even the huge Trans-Space organization. And Porcys had its power all in one place. The planet was organized to the last ounce of energy, if only it could be brought to bear in time.

Dan ordered his anxious companions to take him to Porcys.

Far under the Central City, which was the city he had seen, he found a weary, powerful old man in a light-blue cape and glittering belt, directing operations from a television command post. The console showed street scenes of men in sky-blue capes and flashing belts, who danced and jabbered, their faces aglow with lunacy as they rapped out conflicting orders and the people jerked and dashed this way and that, tears running down their faces.

Near the statue, before the Hall of Truth, close ranks of Porcyn men in orange-and-black capes stood massed on the steps, holding sleek-bored guns. On the street below, gibbering lunatics in sky-blue danced and shrieked orders, but the eyes of the men on the steps were tightly shut. By a technicality, they avoided obedience to the lunacy, for with their eyes shut, how could they be sure who gave the command?

At the belted statue itself, a man in blue was clinging to one bronze arm as he slammed down a hammer to knock loose the partly broken circle. The statue obstinately refused to let go. At the base of the statue, holding a microphone, stood an average-looking man in a sky-blue cape, his lips drawn back in an amused smile. He gestured to men with crowbars and they tried to jam them between the statue and its base. This failing, they took up chisels and hammers. The man working on the circle shrugged and jumped down.

At the console, the old man looked up at Dan. He put his hand out and felt Dan's belt. Apparently the tingle reassured him and he seemed to accept Dan without further question.

"This is about the end," he said. "When that statue goes, those men will feel the jolt and open their eyes. They're the last formed body of troops on the planet, and when they go, we'll have nothing to strike with. There must be something I could devise for this, but I've been up three nights and I can't think."

"Can you delay it?" asked Dan, grappling with the beginning of his plan.

"Oh, we'll delay it. I've got the last of the sweepers collected at the holes opening into the square. Just when that statue begins to tip, I'll let the sweepers out. That will stop things for a while. Then they'll kill the sweepers and my bolt is shot."

"Won't the men you've got here fire on those blue-caped fakes?"

"Devisement," said the old man, shaking his head, "you know better."

"Are there any fire hoses? Will your men squirt water on the blue-caped ones?"

"Yes," said the old man, leaning forward. "They'll get shot. But yes, they will. What is it? What are you devising?"

Dan outlined his plan. The old man's eyes lighted. He nodded and Dan went out and climbed with guides through a grim, dark tunnel where the sweepers were kept. He peered out the hole, and as across the street the statue began to tip, he burst outside and sprinted into the square.

The Trans-Space leader raised his microphone.

Dan ripped it out of his hand and knocked him off his feet, then knelt and picked up the heavy shield that had been taken off the statue to get at the ring.

A bullet hummed over Dan's head.

With a rush of air and a heavy smash, the statue landed full length on the ground. Dan hauled himself up onto its base. Another bullet buzzed past him. Then there was a yell, and Dan looked down in the street.

The sweepers were horrible as they poured from their holes, but they looked almost beautiful to Dan. He glanced at the Porcyns massed on the steps, their faces white with near-hysteria. Their eyes were open and watching him; the Trans-Space men were too busy to give orders.

Dan raised the microphone and his voice boomed out:

"Close your eyes till you hear the roar of the lion! Then obey your true leaders!"

He repeated the order three times before it dawned on the Trans-Space technicians that this was not according to plan. The loudspeaker gave a booming click and cut off. By then, the sweepers had been killed and Dan became aware of bullets thrumming past him. Suddenly he felt weak with panic that the rest of the plan had fallen apart.

Up the street, Porcyn men were unscrewing a cap on the face of a building. They connected a hose. A sky-blue-caped Trans-Space agent ordered them away. The Porcyns turned, wads of wax in their ears, and raised the hose.

A stream of water knocked the agents backward. Shots rang out. Porcyns fell, but other Porcyns took their places. The stream arched and fell on the Trans-Space agents and abruptly a whirl of color tinged the water. Blots and blobs of green, orange, pink and yellow spattered the blue-caped agents.

At the end of the street, someone ran up tugging a lion by the mane.

"*Go*, dog! *Run!*"

Somewhere a child cried out in terror.

The lion roared.

The troops on the steps opened their eyes.

An old man's voice, amplified, spoke out with icy authority:

"*Deploy for street-fighting! First rank, move out along Center Street toward North Viaduct. Rifles at full charge. Wide intervals. Use every scrap of cover. Shoot the false-belted usurpers on sight.*

"*Second rank, move out along West Ocean Avenue toward the sea wall....*"

Shots rang out.

There was a faint thrumming hum, like wires in the wind, and streaks of cherry radiance criss-crossed in the air.

The lion roared, unable to find the child. The roars of other lions joined in.

Dan was aware that he was lying atop the hard base of the statue, but he didn't know how he had come to be there. He tried to stand up.

He heard voices screaming orders, then falling still, and a scene swung into his line of sight like something watched through the rear-view mirror of a turning groundcar.

Half a dozen men, guns in their hands, their bodies and blue capes spattered and smeared till they could hardly be recognized, lay motionless on the pavement

Then the scene swung up and away, and Dan felt weightless. Something hit him hard. His head bounced and he rolled over. Soft grass was in his face. It smelled fresh.

There was a dull boom that moved the ground under him.

He twisted his head to look up.

A massive arm was stretched out over him, its hand firmly gripping the cut edges of a big metal ring.

Somewhere a drum took up a steady monotonous beat.

He fell into a deep black quiet and all the sights and sounds grew smaller and fainter and disappeared entirely.

He awoke in a Porcyn hospital. Kielgaard was there, wearing a broad grin and brilliant Porcyn clothes and promising Dan a huge bonus. But it was all like a dream.

Kielgaard said the Porcyns were as mad as hornets. They had raised a battle fleet and it had taken a corps of diplomats and the Combined Intergalactic Space Fleet to argue them out of personally chopping Trans-Space into fine bits. No one knew what would finally happen, but meanwhile Galactic had its contract and everyone was tentatively happy.

His account finished, Kielgaard grinned more broadly yet and switched on a bedside televiewer.

Dan lifted his head off the pillow and looked at the screen. Then he stared.

It was the statue, solid once more on its base, the ring grasped firmly in one hand and a big wrench in the other. But something seemed different.

Dan at last saw what it was.

It was the face. It wasn't a bad face, if one expected to see strong cheekbones, copper skin and a high-arched nose.

"What a compliment!" he said, embarrassedly pleased. "I—hell, I feel like blushing."

"Make it a good one," said Kielgaard. "After tomorrow, you'll have to blush with your own face again."

"*Tomorrow?*"

"Sure. You're still working for us, remember."

Dan sank back on the pillow and gazed up speculatively at the ceiling. "All right, but I want some time off. I have a fat bonus to spend."

"You could use a holiday," Kielgaard agreed. "Why not try the Andromedan cloud gardens? Pretty expensive, but with your bonus—"

"I've got a place picked out," said Dan. "I'm going to take a vacation on Porcys."

Kielgaard started. "You're joking! Or you've gone twitchy!"

"No. Before I have to give this face back to Surgery, I ought to get a *little* enjoyment out of it. And what could be more enjoyable than hanging around the statue, letting people see the resemblance? Besides, they can't make me take my vacation on the Vacation Planet—I've already had it."

CPSIA information can be obtained
at www.ICGtesting.com
Printed in the USA
LVHW090148031121
702328LV00010B/139

9 789354 599873